DINOSAURS

and all that rubbish   Michael Foreman

PUFFIN BOOKS

0241022347

A man stood on a hill
and looked at a star.
All he thought about,
dreamed about,
was the star.

Grass grew high and trees grew tall.
The man climbed to the top of a tree
and tried to reach the star.
But he was nowhere near it.

The trees filled with birds which flew still nearer the star.
"I must fly," said the man.
"I have money.
I have many men working for me.
I must fly, somehow I must fly."

The man owned some factories nearby.
"Build me a rocket," he ordered.
"Cut down the trees, dig out the coal,
burn whatever will burn,
and build me a rocket
to reach the stars."

All day and all night the fires
in the factories huffed and puffed.
Smoke and fumes and waste and
rubbish poured out and piled up.

At last the rocket was ready,
but there was nowhere for it to be launched.
Everywhere was piled high
with heaps of waste from the factories.

The man took his rocket
to the top of a heap
and set off for the star.

When he landed on the star the man looked about him.
There was nothing to see. He walked and walked,
looking for something to admire.
But still there was nothing.
No trees, no flowers, and not a blade of grass.
Sadly he looked around, but the only thing of wonder
was another star, far off in the black sky.
"I will go to that star," said the man,
and away he went again in his rocket.

On Earth the piles of rubbish smouldered and burned, and the mountains rumbled.

Far below the surface,
the heat disturbed
the sleep of the dinosaurs
who had lain hidden away
for hundreds of years.

They heaved and stretched.
The earth cracked,
and out came
all sorts of
creatures.

A dinosaur held his nose
as he looked around.
"POOH!" he said.
"There is nothing on this
planet but mess.
If we are going to live here
we'll have to get busy."

Some of the dinosaurs burned rubbish in volcanoes.

Dancing dinosaurs broke up the roads.

As the rubbish was cleared
green shoots appeared,
bursting through cracks
and climbing over old forgotten walls.

Telegraph poles and iron pylons
vanished beneath trailing blossoms,
and a fresh new forest
of flowers and trees spread
like a smile around the world.

And all this time the man was heading for his new star,
unaware that it was the very same planet Earth
he had once left behind him.

He landed in a jungle alive with beautiful plants,
sweet with the scent of flowers,
and filled with the song of birds.
"At last," he said, "I have
found my paradise."

"*Whose* paradise?" said the biggest dinosaur.
"Mine," said the man.
"RUBBISH!" said the dinosaur.
"What do you mean by rubbish?" said the man.
"You can't talk to me like that.
Why, with a head as small as yours
you can't possibly have enough brain
to look after this star."

"Our heads are the same size," said the dinosaur,
"but my heart is much bigger than yours.
If you had been ruled by your heart
instead of your head
you would not have destroyed
this paradise before."

"*I* destroyed it?" said the man. "You mean this is *Earth?*"
"Yes, it is," said the dinosaur.
"But it can't be," said the man.
"It is," said the dinosaur.

The man looked about him and saw
that the dinosaur was right.
"Please may I have a small
part of it back?" he asked.
"Please? Just a hill,
or a tree, or a
flower?"

"No," said the dinosaur.
"Not a part of it,
but all of it.
It is all yours,
but it is also all mine.
Remember that.
This time the earth belongs to everyone,
not parts of it to certain people
but all of it to everyone,
to be enjoyed
and cared for."

"Yes, EVERYONE!" sang the birds and the cats
and the mice and the mammoths, the serpents,
the dodos, and the apes.

"EVERYONE!" came the chorus from all living things.

"EVERYONE! EVERYONE!"